Dear Parents:

Children learn to read in stages, and all children develop reading skills at different ages. **Ready Readers**™ were created to promote children's interest in reading and to increase their reading skills. **Ready Readers**™ are written on two levels to accommodate children ranging in age from three through eight. These stages are meant to be used only as a guide.

Stage 1: Preschool-Grade 1
Stage 1 books are written in very short, simple sentences with large type. They are perfect for children who are getting ready to read or are just becoming familiar with reading on their own.

Stage 2: Grades 1-3
Stage 2 books have longer sentences and are a bit more complex. They are suitable for children who are able to read but still may need help.

All the **Ready Readers**™ tell varied, easy-to-follow stories and are colorfully illustrated. Reading will be fun, and soon your child will not only be ready, but eager to read.

Dear Kids:
You must help Billy, Jodie, and their pals! Look at the pictures in
each story then choose the right answer to what happens next!
Every page is a question that must be answered!

WHAT'S NEXT, BILLY AND JODIE?

Illustrated by Becky Radke

Modern Publishing
A Division of Unisystems, Inc.
New York, New York 10022

Waking Up

Billy yawns and stretches.

He kicks off the covers.

What's Next?

He builds a castle.

He gets out of bed.

He gets the cookie jar.

Getting Washed

Jodie washes her face.

She brushes her teeth.

What's Next?

She combs her hair.

She sets the table.

She takes a nap.

Eating Breakfast

Billy drinks his juice.

He eats his cereal.

What's Next?

He gets out of bed.

He wipes his mouth.

He kicks off the covers.

Playing in the Yard

Billy's dog, Skippy, chews on his bone.

He digs a hole in the ground.

What's Next?

Skippy buries his bone.

Skippy jumps into the car.

Skippy shakes himself dry.

Tea Party

Jodie sets the table.

She seats her dolls.

What's Next?

She brushes her teeth.

She washes her face.

She pours the tea.

Nap Time

Jodie takes off her shoes.

She climbs into bed.

What's Next?

She combs her hair.

She takes a nap.

She sets the table.

Building Blocks

Billy gets his blocks.

He empties them on the floor.

What's Next?

He builds a castle.

He gets the cookie jar.

He drinks his juice.

Snack Time

Jodie pours the milk.

Billy gets the cookie jar.

What's Next?

Billy builds a castle.

Jodie seats her dolls.

They sit down and eat their snack.

Flying a Kite

Billy takes his kite to the park.

He ties a long tail on his kite.

What's Next?

Billy finds Jodie's friend, Debbie under the bed.

Billy rides around and around.

Billy watches his kite fly.

Playing Catch

Billy and his best friend, Tommy
put on their baseball gloves.

Tommy tosses the ball.

What's Next?

Billy covers his eyes and counts to ten.

He ties a long tail on his kite.

Billy catches the ball.

Hide and Seek

Billy closes his eyes and counts to ten.

Debbie hides.

What's Next?

Billy buys a ticket for the ferris wheel.

Billy finds Debbie under the bed.

Billy puts on his baseball glove.

Time for Bed

Skippy is tired.

He gets into his basket.

What's Next?

He buries his bone.

He goes to sleep.

He gets his leash.

DID YOU PICK THE RIGHT PICTURE TO FINISH EACH STORY?

Waking Up

Billy yawns and stretches.

He kicks off the covers.

He gets out of bed.

Getting Washed

Jodie washes her face.

She brushes her teeth.

She combs her hair.

Eating Breakfast

Billy drinks his juice.

He eats his cereal.

He wipes his mouth.

Playing in the Yard

Billy's dog, Skippy, chews on his bone.

He digs a hole into the ground

Skippy buries his bone.

Tea Party

Jodie sets the table.

She seats her dolls.

She pours the tea.

Nap Time

Jodie takes off her shoes.

She climbs into bed.

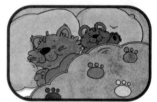

She takes a nap.

Building Blocks

Billy gets his blocks.

He empties them on the floor.

He builds a castle.

Snack Time

Jodie pours the milk.

Billy gets the cookie jar.

They sit down and eat their snack.

Flying a Kite

Billy takes his kite to the park.

He ties a long tail on his kite.

Billy watches his kite fly.

Playing Catch

Billy and his best friend, Tommy put on their baseball gloves.

Tommy tosses the ball.

Billy catches the ball.

Hide and Seek

Billy closes his eyes and
counts to ten.

Debbie hides.

Billy finds Debbie under the bed.

Time for Bed

Skippy is tired.

He gets into his basket.

He goes to sleep.